CW00958044

To John, Philip and Jonah. Thank you for being my inspiration.

Copyright 2021 Stefanis Michailidi

ISBN: 9798518335356

Who am I: The Monkey

by Stefanis Michailidi

My home is high up in the trees
And I hide behind the greenest of leaves

The branch is always my favorite bed
Where I rest my very hairy, brown head

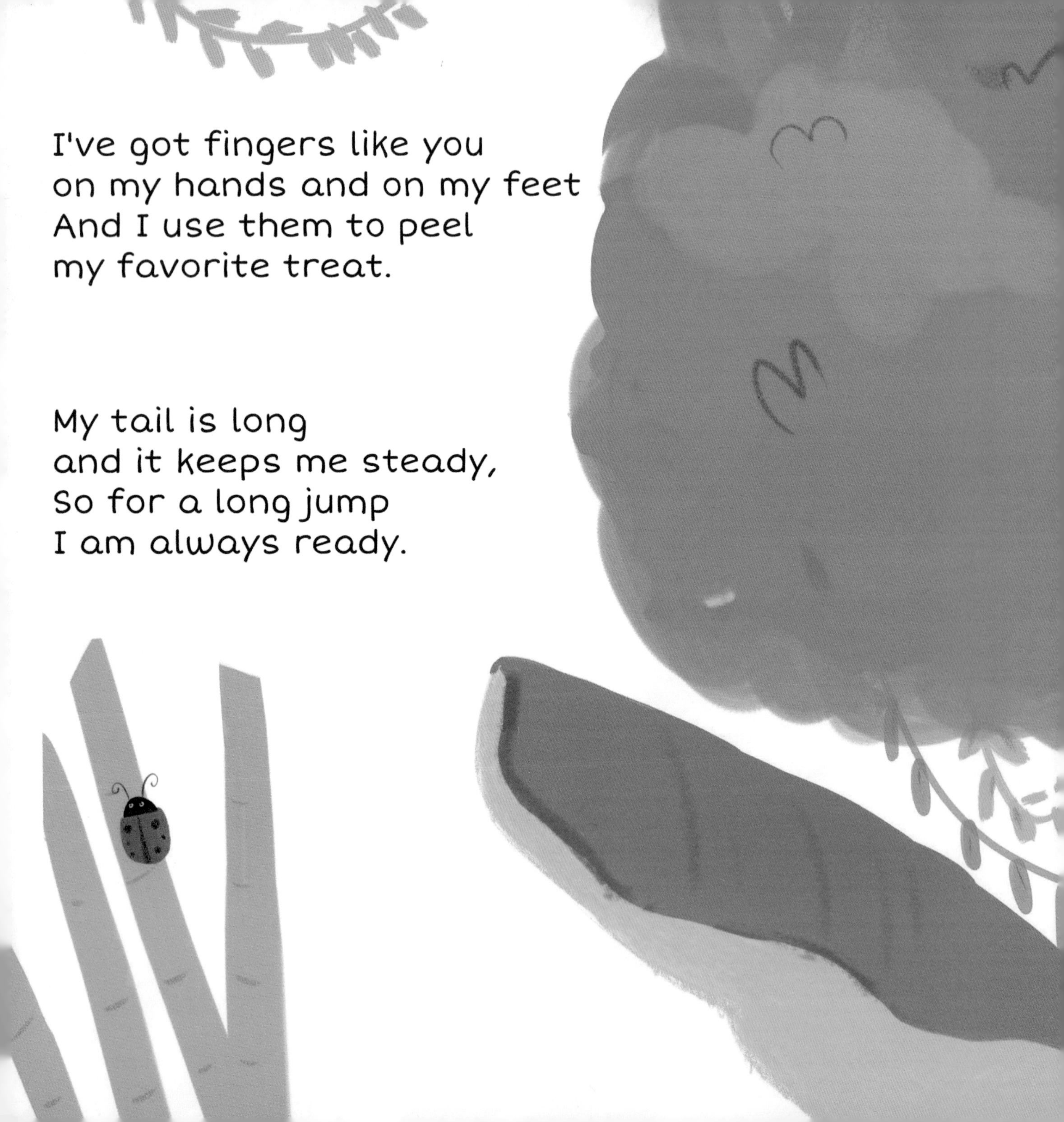

I've got fingers like you
on my hands and on my feet
And I use them to peel
my favorite treat.

My tail is long
and it keeps me steady,
So for a long jump
I am always ready.

When I was a baby my mama breastfed me
We cuddled and hugged, and she would protect me

Now that I am older she tells me to freeze
Whenever she wants to pick off my fleas

But this is so hard for me to do
As I want to play all day just like you

I want to spend
all my time in the sun
And not be bothered
by anyone

I like so much to run around free
And jumping high from tree to tree

Me and my friends take turns in line
So we can all swing from vine to vine

Monkey tricks are
our favorite game
And then we just have
each other to blame

we tickle our tummies
and have lots of fun
and now you think
I would be done...

But no, I keep searching for ventures to do
In the mighty jungle there are always a few

I like to hide well and not make a sound

And then I go

AAAAAAA

and scare
the birds around

Now I see something small
that moves nearby
It is a little lizard
that just caught my eye

And so my lovely days
go by like this
My jungle life you see,
is always bliss

So you have probably guessed
what I might be
I am the cheeky smiley monkey
that sits on a tree.

I am very excited you got this book as this is my first printed story.
I hope you enjoy reading it again and again :)

Stefanis

Printed in Great Britain
by Amazon